W9-BKO-352

STORY BY

Jacqueline Briggs Martin

ILLUSTRATED BY

Susan Gaber

Orchard Books New York

Orchard Books, 387 Park Avenue South, New York, NY 10016

Manufactured in the United States of America. Printed by General Offset Company, Inc.
Bound by Horowitz/Rae. Book design by Mina Greenstein.
The text of this book is set in 16 point Usherwood Medium. The illustrations are watercolor reproduced in full color. 10 9 8 7 6 5 4 3 2 1

Library of Congress Cataloging-in-Publication Data
Martin, Jacqueline Briggs. Good times on Grandfather Mountain / by Jacqueline Briggs Martin ; illustrated by Susan Gaber. p. cm.
Summary: Mountain man Washburn insists on looking on the bright side of things, even as disaster after disaster befalls him.
ISBN 0-531-05977-4. ISBN 0-531-08577-5 (lib. bdg.)
[1. Mountain life—Fiction. 2. Optimism—Fiction.] I. Gaber, Susan, ill.
II. Title. PZ7.M363165Go 1992 [E]—dc20 91-17058

For my husband and son,
my father and brothers—
and brothers-in-law—
every one a fine whittler
on his own wood

—J.B.M.

For my father

—S.G.

Old Washburn always looked at the bright side
of life on Grandfather Mountain.
He never worried and he never complained.
"As long as I have a sharp pocket knife,
I can whittle my way out of any trouble," he said.
And he was a fine whittler.
He could make a fiddle out of an old log,
or a spider out of a stick of wood—
he was that good.

When others grouched at the hot sun
or griped about too much rain,
Washburn sat on his porch
and carved spinning tops, walking sticks,
and dancing clowns.
Close by were his cow, Blanche Wisconsin,
his spotted pig, Powderpuff,
his chickens—the Banties and the Leghorns,
and his garden.

But one spring day
Blanche Wisconsin jumped the fence
and went off down the road,
and Washburn couldn't find her.
"I guess she got an itch to travel," he said.
"Anyway, her milk never did make good cheese."

He fed the Banties and the Leghorns
and Powderpuff, the spotted pig.
He weeded the beans
and swept the floors of his cabin.
He whittled smooth the top of the old wooden pail
and turned it over to make a milk-bucket drum.
"A good drum is better than an empty pail," he said.

It wasn't long before Powderpuff,
in a burst of rooting and digging,
pushed her way under the fence
and trotted down the road.
Washburn looked in mudholes and cornfields.
He asked his neighbors.
But he couldn't find a track
or a trace.

“Well, it will be nice to have no pig
rooting up my radishes and my sweetest lettuces,” he said.
He fed the Banties and the Leghorns.
He hoed the corn and washed his dishes.
He whittled drumsticks
out of a fencepost in the pig yard.

One early morning the Banties and the Leghorns
spread their wings into a gust of wind,
flapped over the fence,
and scrambled off across the field.
"Well, anyone would get tired
of scratching around in the dirt all day
and sitting on eggs," said Washburn.
The chickens were not by the frog pond,
under his neighbor's apple tree,
or in the back pasture.
"At least I won't be waked up every morning
by squabbling hens," he said to himself.
"I can carve rhythm clackers and floor pounders
out of the chicken coop door."

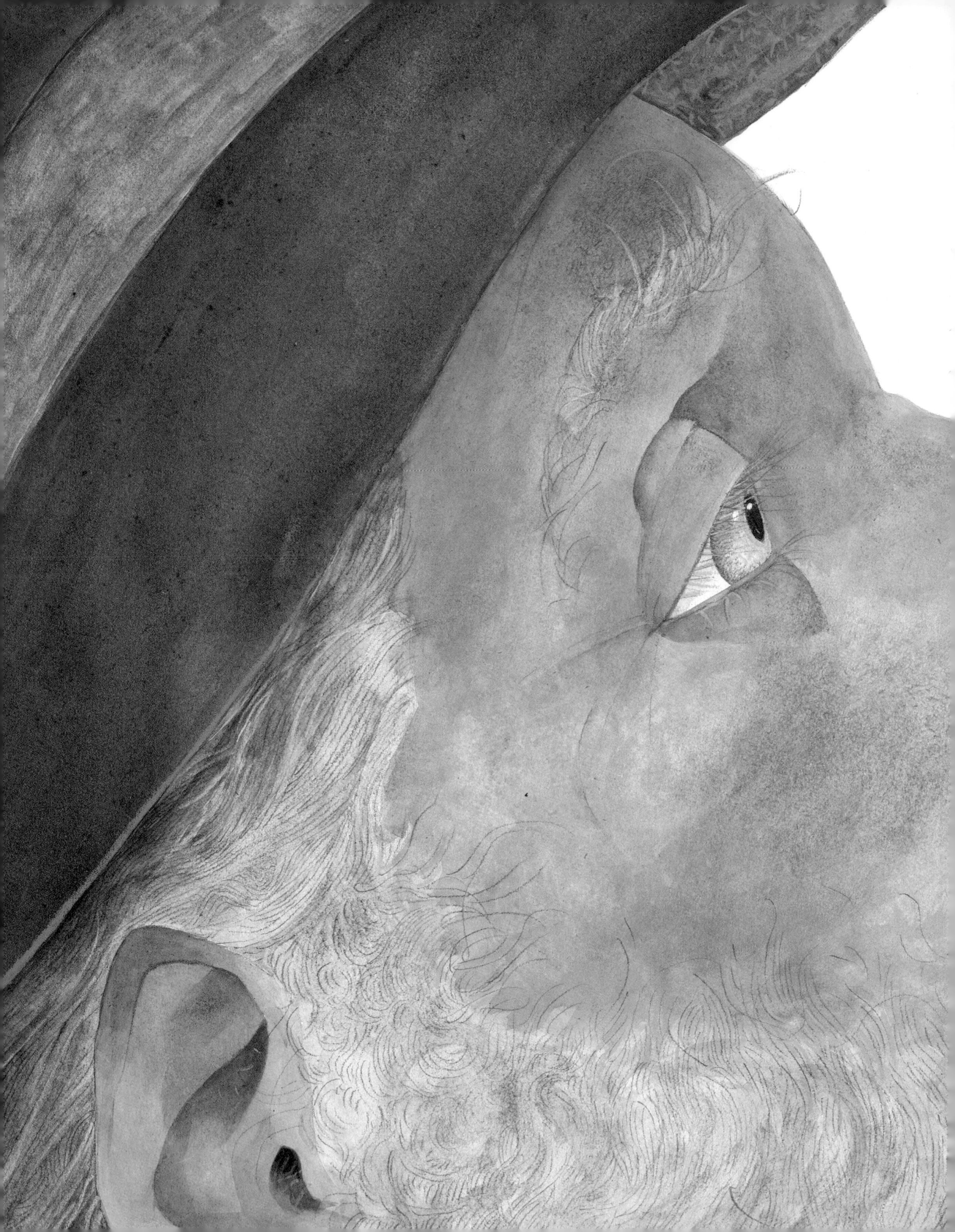

One hot summer afternoon the grasshoppers came
and ate his beans.
"Well, it will be nice not to wear out my back
picking beans," said the old man.
He swept the floors, washed his socks,
and whittled the bean poles into tub thumpers.

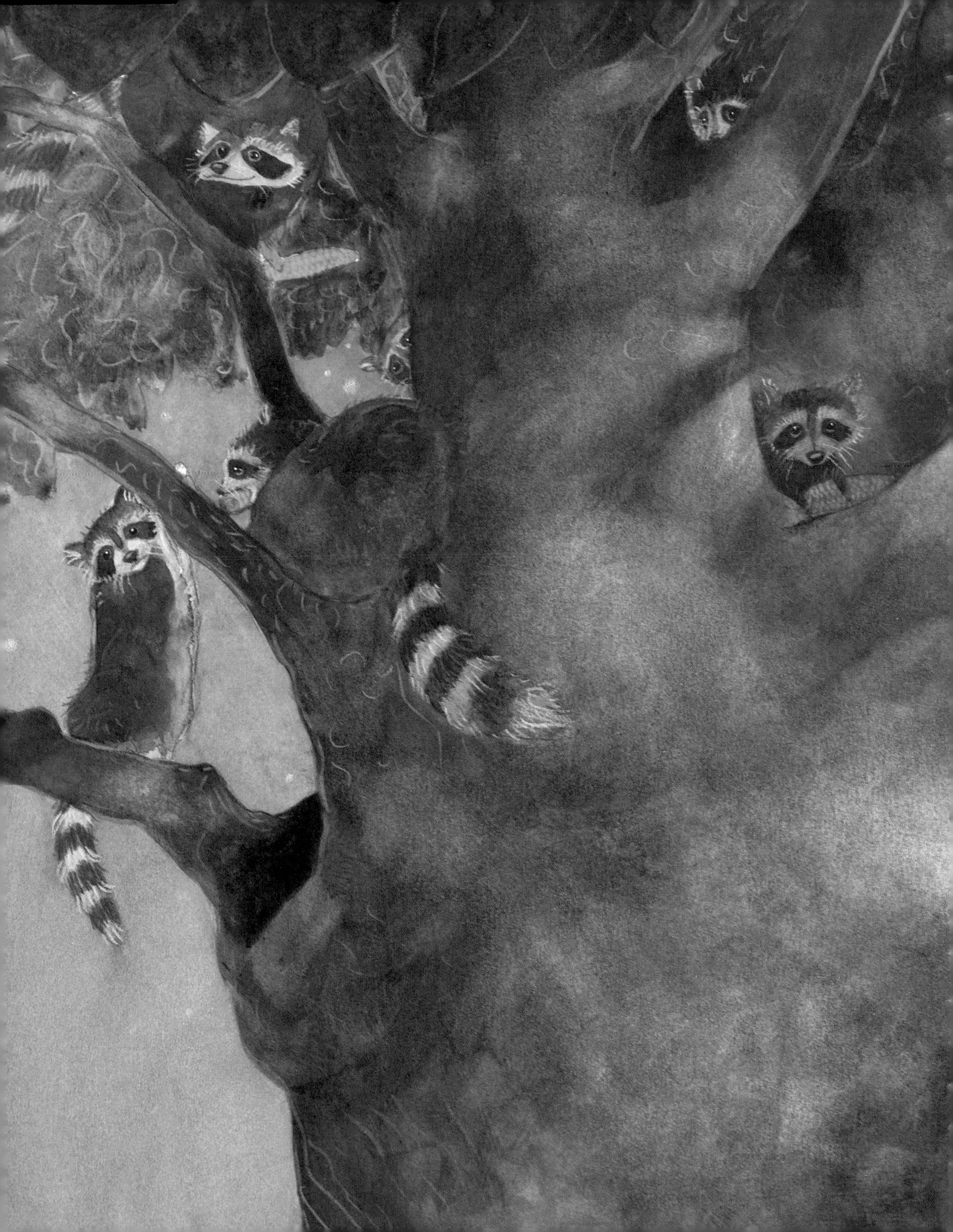

The next week a large family of raccoons
snuck into his corn patch and
ate every ear of corn.
Old Washburn did love sweet corn.
Still, he could see a bright side.
"I have a fine stack of corncobs," he said.
And he decided to make corncob whistles.

A few days later
a fierce mountain storm came through
and blew his cabin down.
"I've slept under stars before," Washburn said.

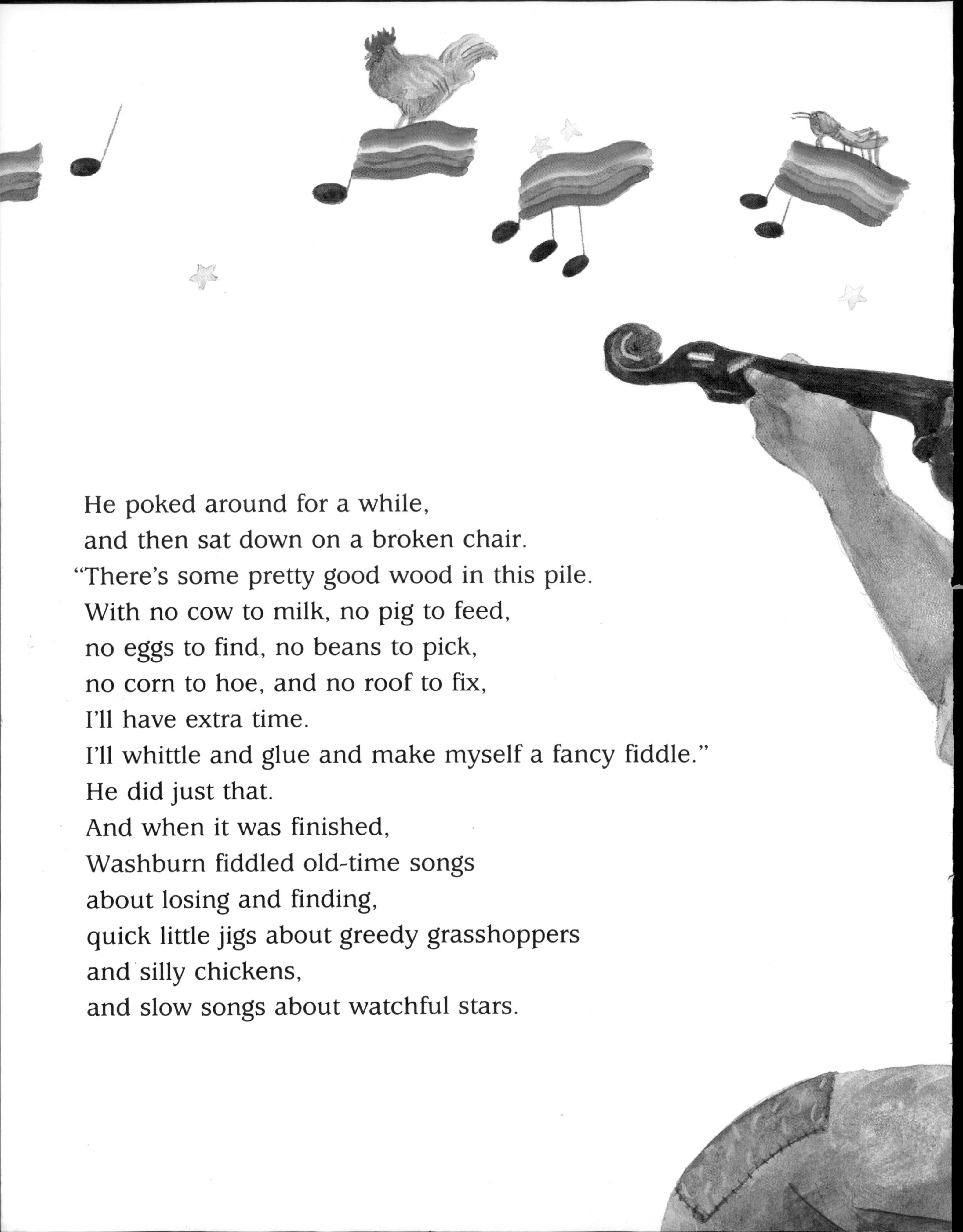

He poked around for a while,
and then sat down on a broken chair.
"There's some pretty good wood in this pile.
With no cow to milk, no pig to feed,
no eggs to find, no beans to pick,
no corn to hoe, and no roof to fix,
I'll have extra time.
I'll whittle and glue and make myself a fancy fiddle."
He did just that.
And when it was finished,
Washburn fiddled old-time songs
about losing and finding,
quick little jigs about greedy grasshoppers
and silly chickens,
and slow songs about watchful stars.

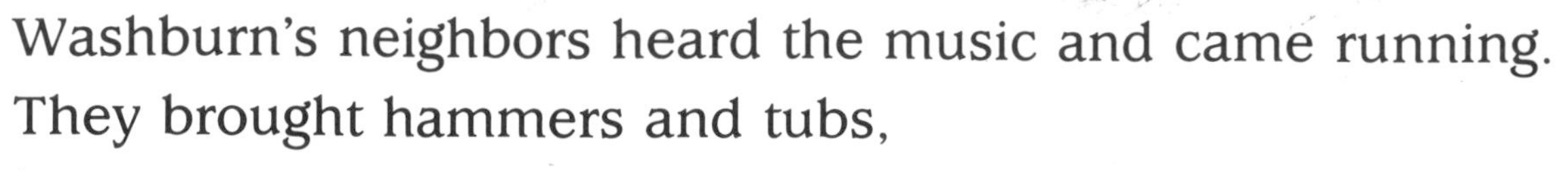

Washburn's neighbors heard the music and came running.
They brought hammers and tubs,
harmonicas and musical saws.
They used Washburn's corncob whistles, floor pounders,
clackers, tub thumpers, drumsticks, and milk-bucket drum.

Washburn and his neighbors danced and laughed
and carpentered on the cabin.
They romped and stomped and played the music
they had learned on Grandfather Mountain.

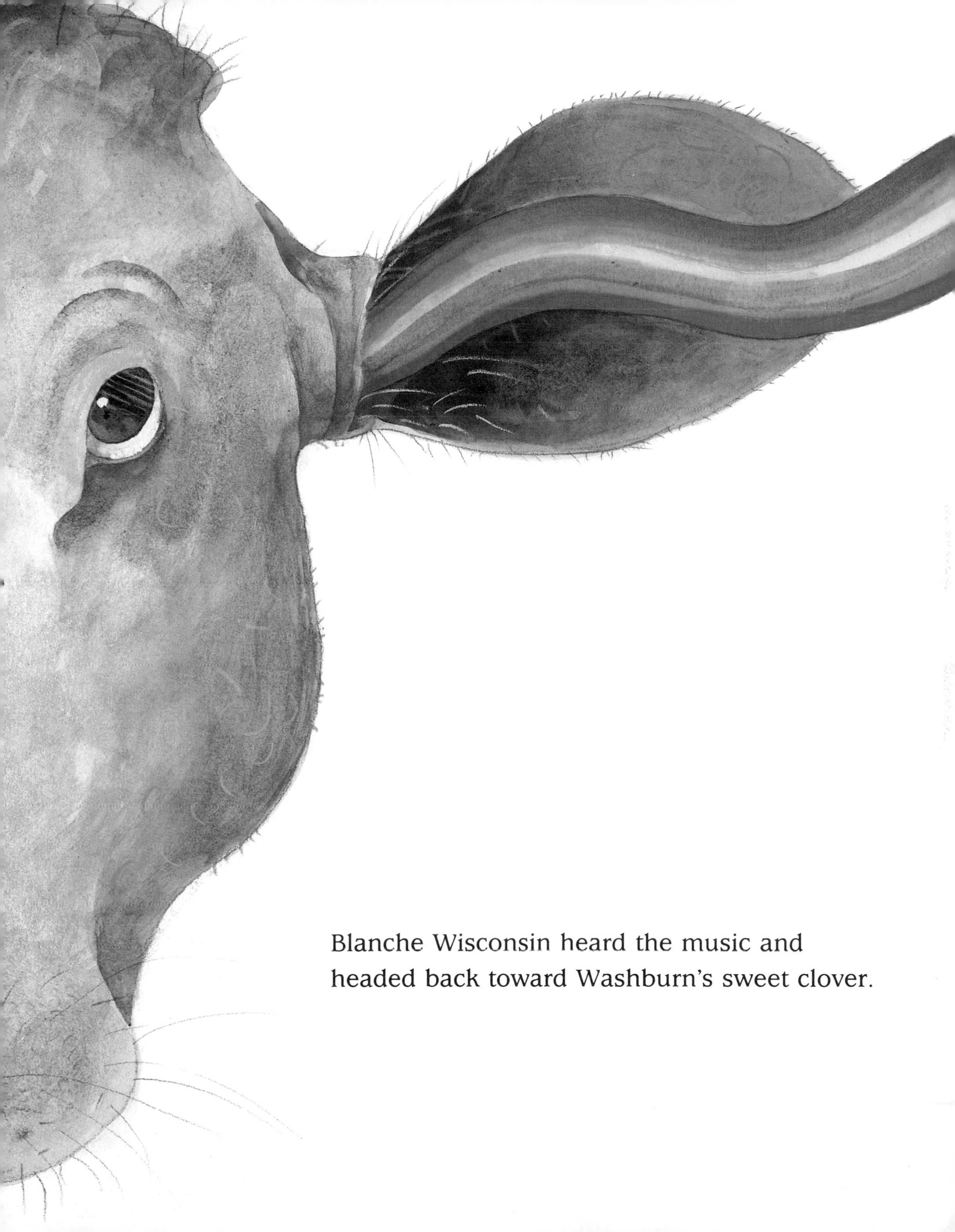

Blanche Wisconsin heard the music and
headed back toward Washburn's sweet clover.

Powderpuff, the spotted pig, heard the music
from the valley and trotted toward the path.
The Banties and the Leghorns heard the music
and hustled back to their old chicken yard
with its mountain crickets and leafhoppers.
The neighbors worked and danced until their shoes fell off.
And they went home singing.

The next morning
Washburn sat on the porch of his fixed-up home.
He looked out at Grandfather Mountain,
his cow, Blanche Wisconsin,
his spotted pig, Powderpuff, the Banties and the Leghorns,
and his new fiddle, hanging on the wall.
He thought of the music, the dancing, and the laughter.
He smiled and hummed a little tune.
Then he pulled out his pocket knife and began to whittle.

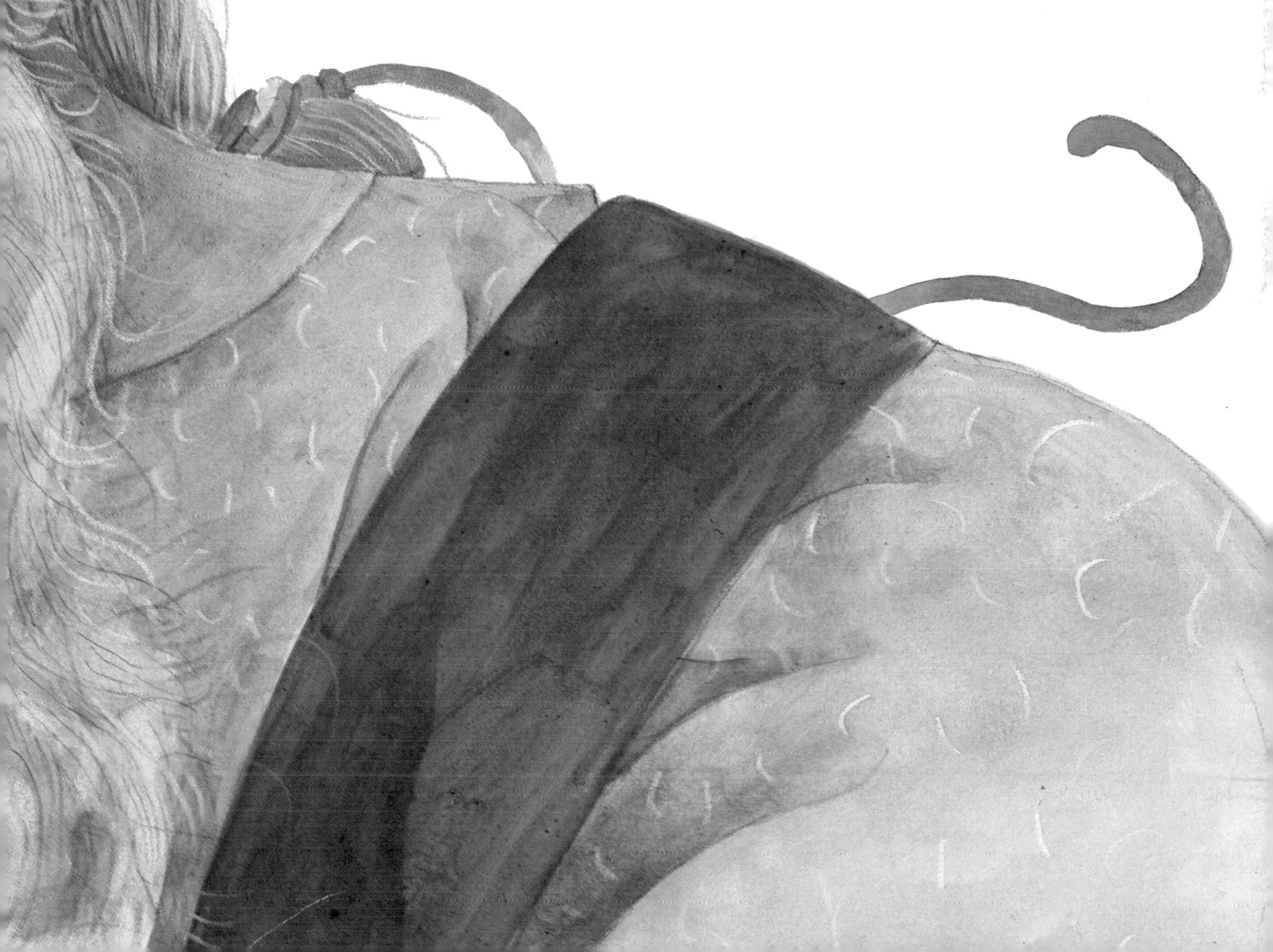

Old Washburn was a fine whittler.
He could whittle a spider out of a stick of wood,
or a party out of a blown-down cabin.
He was that good.